Sing a Song of People

by Lois Lenski

Illustrated by Giles Laroche

HOUGHTON MIFFLIN COMPANY

BOSTON

ATLANTA   DALLAS   GENEVA, ILLINOIS   PALO ALTO   PRINCETON

Acknowledgments

Grateful acknowledgment is made for permission to excerpt and/or
reprint original or copyrighted materials, as follows:

Sing a Song of People, by Lois Lenski, illustrated by Giles Laroche. Text
copyright © 1965 The Lois Lenski Covey Foundation, Inc. Reprinted by
permission of Moses and Singer for the Lois Lenski Covey Foundation,
Inc. Illustrations copyright © 1987 by Giles Laroche. Reprinted by
permission of Little, Brown and Company.

ISBN: 0-395-81433-2

23456789-B-02 01 00 99 98 97

For Andrea and Beth

Sing a song of people
Walking fast or slow;

People in the city,
Up and down they go.

People on the sidewalk,

People on the bus;

People passing, passing,

In back and front of us.

People on the subway
Underneath the ground;

People riding taxis
Round and round and round.

People with their hats on,

Going in the doors;

People with umbrellas
When it rains and pours.

People in tall buildings

And in stores below;

Riding in elevators
Up and down they go.

People walking singly,

People in a crowd;

People saying nothing,
People talking loud.

People laughing, smiling,

Grumpy people too;

People who just hurry
And never look at you!

Sing a song of people
Who like to come and go;

Sing of city people
You see but never know!

SYMBOL

Symbol